Dear Parents:

Congratulations! Your child is taking the first steps on an exciting journey. The destination? Independent reading!

STEP INTO READING® will help your child get there. The program offers five steps to reading success. Each step includes fun stories and colorful art or photographs. In addition to original fiction and books with favorite characters, there are Step into Reading Non-Fiction Readers, Phonics Readers and Boxed Sets, Sticker Readers, and Comic Readers—a complete literacy program with something to interest every child.

Learning to Read, Step by Step!

Ready to Read   Preschool–Kindergarten
• big type and easy words • rhyme and rhythm • picture clues
For children who know the alphabet and are eager to begin reading.

Reading with Help   Preschool–Grade 1
• basic vocabulary • short sentences • simple stories
For children who recognize familiar words and sound out new words with help.

Reading on Your Own   Grades 1–3
• engaging characters • easy-to-follow plots • popular topics
For children who are ready to read on their own.

Reading Paragraphs   Grades 2–3
• challenging vocabulary • short paragraphs • exciting stories
For newly independent readers who read simple sentences with confidence.

Ready for Chapters   Grades 2–4
• chapters • longer paragraphs • full-color art
For children who want to take the plunge into chapter books but still like colorful pictures.

STEP INTO READING® is designed to give every child a successful reading experience. The grade levels are only guides; children will progress through the steps at their own speed, developing confidence in their reading. The F&P Text Level on the back cover serves as another tool to help you choose the right book for your child.

Remember, a lifetime love of reading starts with a single step!

For Mrs. Tettonis, Ms. Natasha,
Ms. Joy, and Ms. Dena, and all the educators and
administrators who work hard every day to make
their students feel welcomed and loved
—A.P.

To Kristina, Nicole, and Karma
for sparking the joy in reading
to future generations
—S.K.

Visit us on the Web!
StepIntoReading.com
rhcbooks.com

Educators and librarians, for a variety of teaching tools,
visit us at RHTeachersLibrarians.com

Library of Congress Cataloging-in-Publication Data
Names: Penfold, Alexandra, author. | Kaufman, Suzanne, illustrator.
Title: Welcome back! / by Alexandra Penfold ; illustrated by Suzanne Kaufman.
Other titles: At head of title: All are welcome
Description: New York: Random House Children's Books, [2023]
Series: Step into Reading. 2, Reading with help | Audience: Ages 4–6.
Summary: Illustrations and rhyming text follow a group of children who learn how
to write, spell, make friends, and be kind on the first day back at school.
Identifiers: LCCN 2022022041 (print) | LCCN 2022022042 (ebook)
ISBN 978-0-593-43004-0 (trade paperback) | ISBN 978-0-593-43005-7 (library binding)
ISBN 978-0-593-43006-4 (ebook)
Subjects: CYAC: Stories in rhyme. | First day of school—Fiction. | Schools—Fiction.
LCGFT: Stories in rhyme. | School fiction. Classification: LCC PZ8.3.P376 We 2023 (print)
LCC PZ8.3.P376 (ebook) | DDC [E]—dc23

Printed in the United States of America
10 9 8 7 6 5 4 3 2 1

This book has been officially leveled by using the F&P Text Level Gradient™ Leveling System.

Random House Children's Books supports the First Amendment and celebrates the right to read.

All Are Welcome

Welcome Back!

by Alexandra Penfold

illustrated by Suzanne Kaufman

Random House 🏠 New York

The sun is up.

The day has begun.

It's back to school

for everyone!

We grab our bags.

We are ready for fun.

We feel excited—
and a little scared.
But we have each other.
We are prepared!

7

We smile and wave.

We meet and greet.

We find our spot.

We take our seat.

We start our morning
with a cheer.

Shout it with me:

ALL ARE WELCOME HERE!

We are here to learn.

We are here to play.

We missed our friends
after a summer away.

We have three things
we keep in mind.

Always try.

Have fun.

Be kind.

There is art to make
and stories to tell.

We will learn to write.

We will learn to spell.

We laugh together.

We hope and dream.

We are all important.

We are all a team.

We are writers.

We are readers.

We are listeners.

We are leaders.

We work.

We share.

We help.

We care.

We are ready for a
new year.

We are all on track.

All are welcome here.

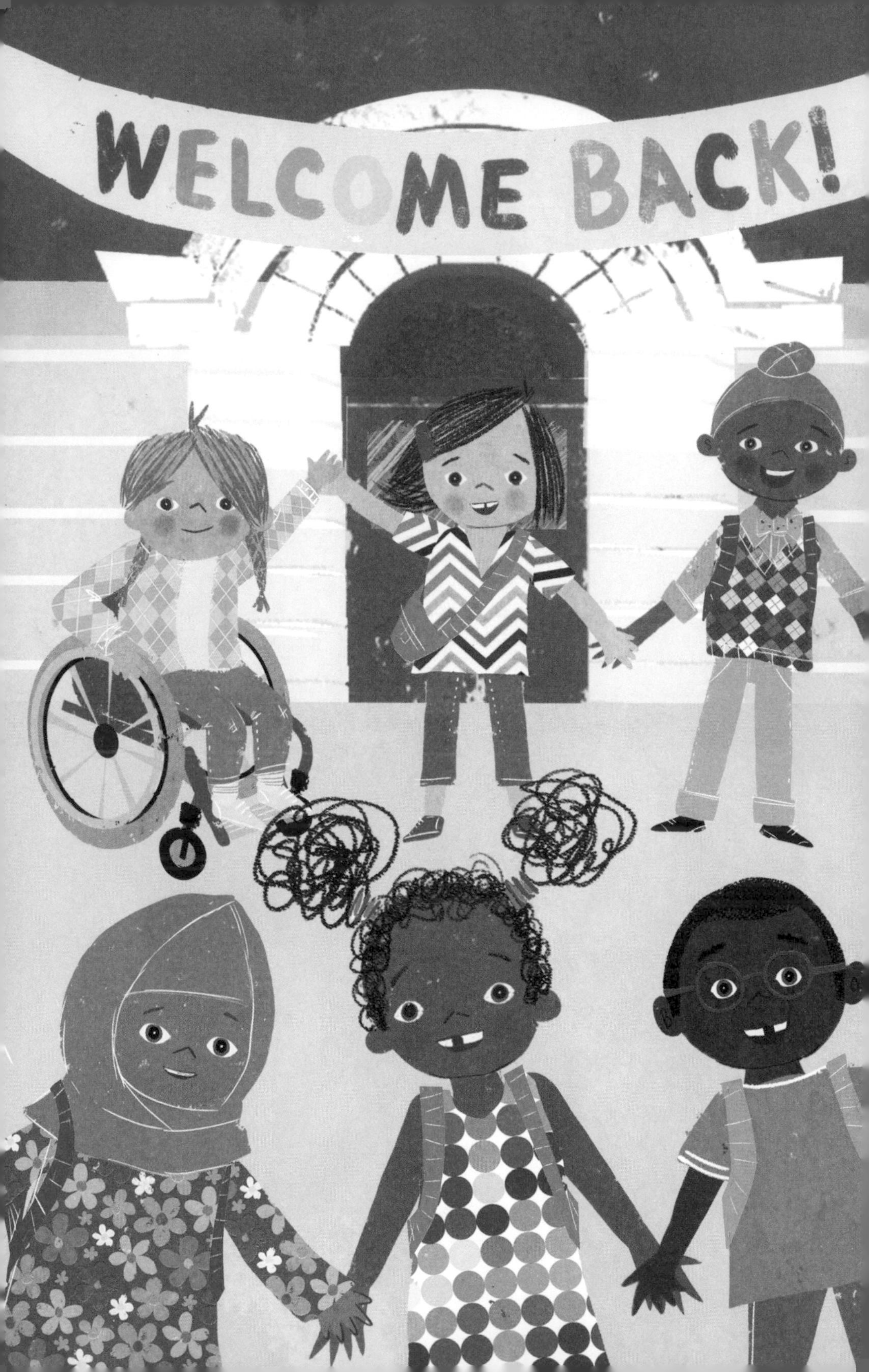
WELCOME BACK!